The Journey of My Life

Krupisa Patel

Author's Picture:

My name is Rupa Patel. I was born in Hathipura village in Gujarat, India. I am Marathi. I have one elder brother. When I was young, my dad passed away. My mom said that my dad was very strict. My mom's family is from Africa. My mom's life was very hard; she had to struggle a lot. Along with my mom, my family came to England after my dad's death in India. My uncle was there, and it was very difficult; my mom had a tough time.

After moving to England, I studied and worked there but struggled a lot. Even though I had the support of my maternal uncle and aunt, as well as my cousin, I felt very lonely. It seemed like everyone was asking why my dad was not there. Everyone said that he had come and done everything for me, but now it was just me left to take care of everything.

My mom has six sisters and one brother. When my mom was young, my grandfather brought my mom and my two aunts from Africa to India. My mom grew up living with her uncle. My mom's uncle was very nice, but her aunt was not very nice and gave my mom and my two aunts a hard time. My mom had a very hard life. Since my mom was three years old, she and my two aunts lived with her uncle and grew up there in India. My daddy remarried my mommy. My mom's marriage was tough; she faced a lot of hardship. My mom's childhood was filled with sorrow.

In England, we moved there and studied everything, but I didn't like it much. Actually, we were young then, but we had a hard time there too while living with uncles. I was studying there with my mom and brother. When we reached college, I and my friend were the only girls among four boys. We had a circle of six friends. We would go to the park together on Sundays to hang out. I don't even know where my childhood ended; time passed in work and study, and I lost track of both. I always played with boys since childhood; I was comfortable around them. Maybe that's because I had a habit of gossiping, and I used to shy away from things I didn't like since childhood. That's why there were more boys in our friend circle.

After moving to England, my uncle told me that he had made arrangements for me and my brother. But at that age, after a short while, memories faded. My childhood had passed, and I was left with a sense of longing. I had a relationship with a boy, but maybe it was not meant to be. I was 20 years old. I was so occupied with studies and work that I didn't realize where the time went. My mom called me back to India. I didn't want to go, but I had to.

When I went to India, on the first and third days, I had to meet potential suitors. The times were such that there was no concept of love marriages. Even in the 21st century, people in India have an old-fashioned mindset. Boys were given freedom, but girls had no freedom. My mom and my family decided on a boy named Shivam for my marriage. I had never met him before, but my marriage was fixed with him.

It felt like my dreams had shattered. I had always dreamed of a love marriage and a partner who would be nice. But now, it felt like my life was falling apart. I wondered why my dad was not around to guide me. After marriage, I moved to my husband's house in the U.S., where things were very difficult. My in-laws were not supportive, and I faced a lot of issues.

I felt like a servant in my own home. Even though I cooked for everyone, it was never good enough. I was constantly criticized and felt isolated. My husband was also not supportive. I had no one to talk to, and every day was a struggle. It felt like my life was being ruined.

Eventually, I became pregnant. The news of my pregnancy gave me some hope and joy. I thought that perhaps life would change for the better with the arrival of my baby. When I gave birth to my daughter on October 3rd, 1995, everything changed. Holding my baby in my arms made everything else seem insignificant.

All my sadness and struggles seemed to vanish with the joy of my daughter's birth. My life was now focused on her happiness and well-being. I made sure that my daughter would not face the same difficulties that I had. Seeing her brought me immense happiness and hope. I wanted to live my life for her and make sure she had a better future.

Eventually, I decided to return to India to be with my family. After some time, I realized that having another child might bring more joy to our family. I had to adapt to the new environment and face challenges, but I wanted to ensure that my daughter would have a good life.

Even though my life was filled with struggles, I found solace and strength in my daughter. I was determined to give her a better life and make the most of the opportunities that came our way.

I used to handle all the household chores, including cooking, serving guests, and taking care of the family. My husband used to go out with other women, and I felt like I was always left behind. Despite the difficulties, I had to do everything myself. This was my life. I was someone who worked for free. When I became pregnant for the second time, my mom was supposed to come from England for the delivery. I was very happy but also sad. I was sad because I knew that people would not treat my mom well and that they would not treat me well, either. I was distressed thinking about what I would do if people did not treat my mom well.

When my mom arrived, it was as if my only source of comfort was finally here. I felt very lonely in the U.S., where there was no one for me. My husband's entire family was there, but I felt like I was alone. My husband was spending time in the hotel because he enjoyed it there and preferred to stay with everyone rather than work at home. My in-laws used to make my mom do all the household work.

As time passed, my mom was working at my in-laws' house, and my baby's arrival was near. The doctor told me that I would either live or my baby would, because my baby was in a breech position. The doctor suggested that I needed to be admitted to the hospital and undergo an induction to deliver the baby. So, I was admitted to the hospital, and the doctor performed an induction to deliver the baby. I gave birth to my second daughter. My mother-in-law started complaining about my having another daughter and how she had hoped for a son.

When my second daughter was born, my father-in-law in India told my brother that my daughter had given birth to another daughter, and it was still not a son. Even in the 21st century, people still prefer sons. This mindset made no sense to me. Even though I was thankful to have another daughter, my father-in-law was unhappy with the birth of another daughter. My mother-in-law and father-in-law were disappointed because they had hoped for a son.

My father-in-law thought that having another daughter was a disappointment, and my mother-in-law continued to treat my mom badly. Despite my efforts, it felt like nothing could change their mindset. My mom remained quiet because, in Indian culture, daughters are expected to be silent and accept the situation. Even when faced with disrespect, my mom chose to remain silent.

As time went on, the situation did not improve, and my husband's behavior became increasingly difficult to handle. My mother was with me for six months, and during that time, I found solace in the company of my daughters. However, even though my mother was there, I felt isolated and misunderstood. My father-in-law continued to express dissatisfaction with having granddaughters instead of grandsons.

Eventually, my time with my mother came to an end, and she left. I was left to deal with the situation on my own, and despite all the challenges, I had to continue living with the difficulties of my life. My daughters were my only source of comfort and strength, and I continued to focus on their well-being despite the obstacles I faced.

For three years, I had been trying to conceive, and then I got a call from my in-laws in India saying that this time, for the third time, we would have to try again. My in-laws insisted that I should have a boy this time, and that if I had a girl, it would be a problem. They made it clear that they only wanted a boy and didn't care if I had to go through the process again. In this era, everyone is busy with their own lives, and people don't understand the emotional toll this puts on others. My in-laws pressured me so much that they even told my husband that I had to bring a boy this time. It was a form of blackmail, and I felt helpless because I wasn't able to go to England.

I didn't want to be a burden on anyone, and I was aware that having a girl was something I had to accept. I knew that having a child wasn't going to be easy, and even though I was aware of it, I felt a lot of pressure from all sides. My family members took one side, and I was left alone. I had no friends, no relatives; I was isolated and felt like a failure. Despite the pressure and expectations, I eventually got pregnant for the third time. When I went to the doctor, I had an ultrasound, but the news didn't seem to be in my favor.

The doctor told me that the decision of whether to keep the baby or not was up to my husband and me. My husband was called in, and the doctor told him that we were expecting a girl. I was devastated. I knew my in-laws would be upset because they wanted a boy, and the disappointment was palpable. Even though I was aware that a girl wasn't what my in-laws wanted, I had to accept it. When the delivery time came, my in-laws arrived for the delivery, expecting a boy, but it turned out to be a girl.

I had to face their disappointment. My in-laws were very cold towards me and did not show any affection or support. They didn't even acknowledge my daughter, and I felt like I was treated as less important. My father-in-law didn't care, and it was painful to see how my daughter was treated. My husband and in-laws were more concerned with what society would think than with my well-being or the well-being of my child.

My daughter wasn't even looked at properly, and on top of that, I was told that I gave birth to a stone, as if it was entirely my fault. Their son was blameless in their eyes. When guests came to see Sita, everyone stayed quiet and said nothing. Even my sister-in-law came, but I wasn't speaking to anyone; I was just taking care of my three daughters. My father-in-law was so cruel that even when my little Sita cried, he didn't like it. How could that little angel understand that her grandfather didn't like her at all? How could I explain to that little fairy in which house she had been born? I didn't know if it was my daughter's bad luck or mine. I couldn't understand how the days were passing.

As time went on, Sita turned one month old, and my in-laws decided to go back to India. My husband was supposed to drop them off at his sister's house. To be honest, I was very happy. I had no idea what life was playing with me. I missed my mom and dad terribly, and I kept thinking, if only my dad were here, would I even be in this situation? I would have married the man I loved and been happy. But here I was, trapped in a life I didn't want.

There was nothing I could do because I didn't have U.S. residency, and my husband didn't have it either. He had Canadian residency. Kriti and Rukmini, my first two girls, were very happy that a new baby had arrived in the house. For Rukmini, it was like she had gotten a new toy. When Sita turned one, my husband decided to go to India. I was so relieved, thinking that at least I wouldn't have to wake up every morning to his anger. I knew I would have to manage the hotel guests, my three young daughters, and all the housework on my own, but still, I felt a sense of peace.

My sister-in-law lived next door, but she never helped me, not even once. On top of that, she was always out and about. There were times when my husband called me at 10 PM asking if there was any food left. He would say, 'Jayashree is running late,' referring to my sister-in-law, Jayashree.

After finishing all the work, I would sit down exhausted, only to have to get up again to cook. Many times, I would think to myself, 'Is this why I came here?' Even after doing everything, I didn't get anything in return. Instead, everyone would scold me and say whatever they wanted. I would finish all the work, and then I never received anything in return, and on top of that, everyone would curse me and speak to me however they liked. After finishing all the work and sitting down exhausted, I had to cook again. I couldn't go anywhere or talk to anyone. It felt like these people were of a different kind. If someone keeps a pet in their home, they love the pet. But I was a human, and I often felt like life had become too difficult. Life felt very tough. Many times, I thought it would be better to die, and I would often fall into depression.

It hit me that my in-laws were terrible. They didn't like my daughters, so how could they like me? If something happened to me tomorrow, who would look after my daughters? As time passed, the moment came for my husband to return from India. My in-laws would send sarees and other things from India, but my sister-in-law would take the good ones and give me the bad ones. It was as if I had never seen or worn anything good in my life. Even the parcels would go to my sister-in-law's place, and she would give all the good dresses to her and pass the unwanted ones to me.

There was so much discrimination. When I spoke to my husband about it, he would say, 'There's no need for you to say anything,' and he would talk to me as if I had no right to speak. He said, 'If you don't like it, why doesn't your mother send you anything? What for?' He even told me, 'I feed you and provide for you, don't I?' He wouldn't speak or let me speak.

A woman can endure everything if her husband is on her side, but here, my husband wasn't on my side either. When I tried to speak up, he raised his hand against me. That's the kind of value he had—raising a hand on a woman. That's not manliness, but he thought it made him a man. When he raised his hand, he felt powerful, and I felt like I had to remain silent.

I finally told him, 'There's no need for you to act as if I've never seen clothes before.' I gathered the courage to say it. 'I don't want any clothes from your family, and I'll take care of myself from now on.' I also called my mother-in-law in India and told her about how I was being treated. I said, 'Maybe you don't know, but I don't want any more clothes from you, and you don't need to send anything to me.'

My mother-in-law once told my husband, 'If a heart breaks once, it will never mend again, so be careful of what you're doing.'

Yes, I will say that in the entire family, my mother-in-law was the only one who was a bit kind, but who listened to her? She once told me she would send a separate parcel for me, but I didn't want anything anymore.

It's been eight years since we got married, and in these eight years, I haven't seen anything in the U.S. except his sister and their house. It's been constant fighting every day, no peace at all. I used to think it would be better if the night didn't end. Eight years passed like this, and the fights only got worse. Then, one day, my husband slapped me again and strangled me. I still remember my daughter Kriti standing and holding Sita. Sita started crying, and Rukmini also started crying.

"What is Daddy doing to Mommy?" My three daughters were crying, calling out, "Mom, Mom." In the end, I had to do what I didn't want to. I had to call the police that unfortunate day. My daughters stood there crying, witnessing everything. I couldn't even speak because my throat had been squeezed so tightly. I called the police, and they took pictures of me and arrested Shivam.

I felt pity because I grew up without a father. I yearned for a father's love but never received it. My daughters were still so young, and how could I take away the love of their father, which I never had? My daughters need their father's love, and who will give that to them? That's why I didn't press charges. We returned home with the help of a friend, and even though I wasn't at fault, I apologized—for the sake of my three daughters. The felony charge was reduced to a misdemeanor, and Shivam had to attend anger management classes for a year.

Despite everything, his entire family was angry at me for getting him arrested, but they didn't seem to care about the impact all this had on my three young daughters. They didn't consider what was going through their minds. Instead, they started cursing my mother and questioning her upbringing. They blamed me, cursed me, and made my life unbearable. But I couldn't let them take away my will to live.

Despite my divorce, my ex-husband and I were always on and off for the sake of my daughters. Yes, there was never any physical relationship between us, but I sacrificed my life for my daughters, and I don't regret it at all because what I did was for them. No matter the problems between my ex-husband and me, I wanted my daughters to receive love from their daddy. I did it because it was very necessary. Even after the divorce, living together often felt awkward for me, but when I looked at my three daughters, it felt okay because I did it for them. And yes, I won't lie; the reason I did it was that at least my ex-husband helped my daughters, so I had a little less tension. That's why, even though I didn't like it, I stayed with him. We stayed together for six months, and after separating, my ex-husband would often come back and leave again.

To tell the truth, my life was such a struggle that I had to stay with a person I didn't like at all for the sake of my daughters. Even after the divorce, I had to live with him. My ex-husband would often take my daughter away while I was sleeping.

And I was ready to work as a housemaid at someone's house because I was so desperate for money. That's when I decided I had to work; how long could I go without a job without the right visa? I decided to try for a job in Houston.

Then, I got a job at Sangam Jewelers, a gold store. I started staying with an Indian family at the Hilton, working as a pencase (assistant or helper). I worked six days a week, and I started earning money there. I paid rent every month and continued working.

The other girls would visit their homes, and eventually, we all became friends. I started to enjoy the job a little. However, the store owner had bad intentions toward me, but there were other girls around, so nothing happened. The girls would invite me to their homes for meals, but my heart was always with my daughters. With my earnings, I bought a mobile phone—the first thing I had bought for myself after marriage. I felt proud.

I would call home, but I was rarely allowed to talk for long. I applied for my work rights, but until they were approved, I had no choice but to wait. One day, the jeweler's owner asked me to join him at a hotel. I refused. Seeing a single woman, they all think the same, but I maintained my character. I worked there for six months, but they didn't pay me regularly. The family I stayed with was kind. One day, Shivam's brother came to visit. He was very good-hearted, and after meeting him, Shivam asked me to come back, but I refused. I didn't want to sit idle at home again.

Three more months passed as I listened to songs at the store and had fun with the other girls, who always tried to make me laugh and keep me happy. I will never forget that in my life. Then, one day, Shivam came back and told me about a job at G.M., but it was for a couple. I thought it was a good opportunity. After another month, I returned to Florida and got a job at a hotel.

I worked there during the day, and at night, Shivam worked for two days as well. Since there was no accountant at night, both of our paychecks came as one. Shivam was stingy, but he did buy me the things I needed. I didn't have any Indian clothes or special dresses. In Florida, there was a temple where I made a lot of friends, but I didn't go often because I didn't have proper clothes. My mom had gone to India, so I asked her to bring me some Indian dresses. When she did, Shivam criticized them, saying, 'No one wears these kinds of clothes; they're cheap.' He didn't have the guts to buy me clothes himself. He had no money but always spoke as if he were born with a silver spoon in his mouth. But all his words were false. He had nothing, and before coming to the U.S., he hadn't built anything on his own. He often spoke rudely about my mom as well.

In my fate, there were not one but two bad people. I wanted nothing but love in my life. That was the only thing missing. Nobody in his family liked me, but nobody spoke up because of the constant fighting. He believed that everyone in the house respected him, but that was not true. He always belittled everyone and had no power to give anyone anything. He would talk in such a way that everyone believed him. He was a sweet talker. I had never seen anyone like him in my life. I don't know what life was trying to show me. I couldn't understand anything; everything was beyond my comprehension. I couldn't make sense of what was happening or where I was headed.

Every Sunday, he would take me to the temple. I was working there and noticed an apartment that made me dizzy—such apartments in the U.S.A. had such high rents. I was very scared, but there was nothing I could do; I was helpless. We fought every day. He never spoke to me kindly. He had a short temper. He would abuse and take money from my mother. He would also dominate me and often leave me wondering what God had written for my life. Would I ever find true love or happiness?

He was angry with me. As a mother, I couldn't call my daughters my daughters. He was my husband, but not my boyfriend. Even though he was supposed to support me when I needed help, he would use me. At that house, everyone had a bad opinion of me and wanted to use me. Despite being safe there, I was constantly subjected to hardships. He wanted to show everyone that our marriage was a love marriage, but it wasn't.

He was not even a proper husband. He kept hiding the truth from everyone and pretending everything was fine, but lies only lasted so long before the truth came out. He taught me not to tell anyone anything. I stayed with him, only going to the temple, where everyone was nice to me, but his actions made me feel degraded.

Though I made friends at the temple and it felt somewhat good, his behavior was damaging. He always talked about how he owned hotels and had such grand stories, but I didn't like lying. I couldn't speak up, so he kept silencing me. Many people worked in jobs, but he thought that speaking falsely was acceptable. He hardly ever spoke the truth in his life. He would constantly belittle my daughters, and I felt like dying. I wanted to speak out but couldn't. Everywhere I went, he would only talk about God, but reading the Bible doesn't mean practicing it. Talking about something doesn't mean you're good at it. He was an expert in talking but lazy in action. Over time, I learned about his family and how his mother called him a demon. My husband wasted 200 tolas of gold and all my diamonds and jewelry. To this day, I don't know what he did with them. He even took my phone calls, telling me it was all lies. He was a very bad person.

My husband and I had a very strained relationship. He would often say that my family didn't matter, and his indifference made the situation worse. I felt isolated and unsupported. I faced a lot of domestic abuse and violence from my husband, which was very distressing. Even when I tried to seek help or voice my concerns, it was often met with aggression or neglect.

Eventually, I reached a breaking point when my husband physically assaulted me in front of my children. The police were involved, and I had to face the legal consequences of the situation. Despite my efforts to protect my children and myself, the emotional and physical trauma was immense. I felt that my family and my in-laws were not supportive and that my life had become unbearable.

I struggled with the separation from my children, and the legal battles that followed were exhausting. My in-laws and husband continued to disregard my feelings and needs, and the entire experience left me feeling dejected and broken. Despite the support I received from some friends, the emotional toll of the situation was significant. My life had become a constant battle for survival and dignity, and it was challenging to find peace or happiness.

In the end, I was left with a deep sense of loss and despair. My dreams of a supportive family and a happy life seemed distant, and I had to navigate a difficult path with minimal support and understanding from those around me.

I didn't know that Ram would come into my life as a blessing, moving forward. My brother, my guru, I believe in him. We went to his house, where my heart wasn't willing to go. I didn't want to go to New Orleans, and my friend here said that I should go with this man. He said, "We'll call your friends over for a visit because my Green Card situation was still uncertain." Although I was somewhat calm after receiving the approval letter, I still wasn't clear about everything. I received a call from him, and another reason for not going was that my daughters were here, so I would get to see them.

I didn't see much in New Orleans, as nothing was available on the Internet either, so I just went, did my part, and then we proceeded slowly. Since then, I have never been outside the house. We came here, and Ram worked hard in many ways. As usual, he warned me not to mention the girls' names. He was not married to me, but my proximity made it difficult for him to say no. His wife, Lalita Ben, was very kind. She had made delicious food and served it. She had also prepared an elaborate dinner.

When I first went to their house, it felt like we had never met before. It felt like visiting our own home. The people I met in my life were really nice, and I felt that God had prepared everything well in advance for me. After eating, we talked about India, and I stayed overnight. The next morning, Lalita Ben made a hot breakfast and even packed food for the road. She said that other friends of theirs would come to meet us on the way, so we should join them for lunch. The lunch was very nice, and after spending some time there, we left. The road was quite deserted. Seeing it, I felt unsure about what lay ahead, but as we drove closer, we arrived at the hotel where we were supposed to work.

In New Orleans, the place where we stayed was a native Indian area. All the hotel rooms were occupied, and we were given an apartment. Though the apartment had nothing in it, the expenses were covered by the hotel. We started working slowly and setting up everything in a standard manner. On the second day, we went to the town, which was devoid of any stores or Walmart; it was very desolate. The altitude was around 12,000 feet, and everyone who came here was either a casino person or a native Indian.

The hotel was run by native Indians, and though there were a few people working there, many left their jobs. I also had to make some changes in the hotel and hire new people. Gradually, I adjusted to the work and began to like it. Even though I was from India, the native Indians had an allergy to other Indians. They spoke poorly of their own people and thought they were the only good ones.

The town had a small family of Indians, but they did not like anyone or interact with anyone. I was in the same situation and tried to maintain my character well. The owner was not happy with anyone and had a very bad nature. They always had problems with people and created issues with everyone they interacted with. I was just doing my job and did not bother much about their behavior.

One day, I had to attend a convention in a nearby city. We had to travel and deal with a lot of problems related to the hotel. During my time there, my mother came from England to visit. She liked the place, but my brother and sister-in-law, who were visiting America for the first time, had some trouble adjusting.

They had to open a bank account and transfer forty thousand dollars. My sister-in-law was very kind and helped set everything up. She didn't want to interfere with my husband's ways. My sister-in-law's family had their own troubles but were supportive. We went to a temple and met new people who were very kind. I felt more comfortable and connected with them.

In New Orleans, we had some issues, and my mother's family had to leave. My husband's younger brother, Rohan, was a good person but had problems with alcohol and was not always reliable. Despite everything, I managed to maintain my composure and adapt to the situation. Eventually, I learned to manage my life there and made the best of it.

There, my brother was thinking of coming back and visiting me. Of course, my brother asked me a question about the money that was transferred into the account when he was in America and opened the account. At that time, I couldn't say anything about the money because I was in a tight spot. But everyone who came into our lives took advantage of me. My brother said that he knew it wasn't my fault, but he wanted to open the account with his wife. So I couldn't do anything, but during a time of destruction, I lost my mind, and my sister-in-law didn't listen to me and got manipulated by a sweet-talking person, leading to the money being taken away.

In my life, I've never hurt anyone, even though everyone hurt me so much. I always prayed to God, "What goes around comes around." But yes, I did hurt one person very much.

First, my ex took all the money my brother gave and took everything from me. I know I should never have done that; it's not good to say such things. But when someone has hurt you so much, words just automatically come out, like when my dad was taken away by God at a young age, and I never received any love from anyone.

Because of circumstances, I had to keep my daughters at his house for some time. I don't know for whom God did what He did, but whenever something bad was going to happen, I could always sense it. Then my husband came with me, taking the girls, and I did what I had to do. It was a very small town, but it was very beautiful. It took years to get to L.A. from there, but the journey was enjoyable because there were Indian stores and Indian restaurants. My friend worked in a salon there, so I used to go there shopping, and after wandering around, I would come back with my daughters.

How we got a hotel license, Ganesh also knew about it, and when we took the hotel, Ganesh was in India. It was a small town, and the hotel there wasn't in good condition. So we went to town, wandered around, and then decided to take it. The hotel was previously run by a homeless man who used to drive a motorbike. I handled everything myself after taking over the hotel. There was no helpline, so I learned everything on my own. Then, one day, I felt that this man was bad. After a little time, I learned everything, and within a week, I fired him. After firing him, I hired new people, and then I remembered my friend, who was in New Orleans, so

I called her and offered her a job. But the problem was that my ex was also the same way as before.

My friend moved to Texas, and after that, we gave her an apartment. We moved into a condo, and she was staying in the apartment and running the hotel. I got along well with her because we got along well from the start. My ex didn't like her, and he started listening to me again, just like before. It felt like this man had changed a bit. I used to get angry because he kept telling me that neither my brother nor my sister-in-law should work here, and he also used to say that I didn't work either. But I was the one running the hotel, not him.

Anyway, after Riddhima left, I was happy, and my daughters were with me. We went to the temple and ate at the restaurant. We then went to Gondal, which cost 160,000. She worked with me for three months, then had to leave because her aunt had cancer, and no one was there to take care of her. So, she left, and her son came along. Then, her daughter also came, and all of them knew me from New Orleans. I wouldn't lie; we worked at the hotel and also flipped houses, and we were happy. But one day, my ex got into a fight with her, acting like a chameleon. Honestly, I felt like slapping him. Then, one day, he told me that he couldn't work anymore. To be honest, all the people I met in my life turned out to be psychos, and when he said that, I felt like he was the same.

After that, she moved back to Texas, and all the work fell on my shoulders. He didn't even know how to use a computer. I started working from 7:00 AM to 11:00 PM, but I enjoyed it. The hotel was renovated completely, and most of the people there were homeless. I gradually kicked them all out, cleaned up everything, and kept working. I kept finding new people, but they would leave. There was one front desk girl whom I hired and trained. I went to the restroom for 15-20 minutes, and when I came back, she had left. It was a new experience for me in training. There weren't any special people there.

I gave an advertisement in an Indian newspaper, and many people came and went, but no one who could work well. Only people who came to pass the time. Then, a lady came, but she also left because of her nature. I just couldn't get along with her. However, there was one nice housekeeper who worked the breakfast shift in the morning. Because of her, I didn't have to wake up at 6:00 AM anymore. She helped me a lot in the morning, but she had problems too. But yes, she worked because of me.

One day, a couple came from Argentina. There was a man named Chris who lived there, and he needed work, so I hired him. I felt a little peace after that. One of the housekeeper's daughters passed away, and then a man named Heath came with his wife. But problems started with him too, and I was so tired of working alone 24/7 that one day, I was so exhausted that I prayed to God. From childhood until now, not a single day has passed in my life without some problem or another. I don't even have peace on one side. Every day I pray to God to give me death because I can't bear it anymore. Then my mom called, and she said that Kriti called, and I felt so relieved. Yesterday, I told my mom that all this was happening, so I was talking to her and my daughters. I used to talk to them before as well. When I talked to my mom, she gave the phone to Kriti, and Kriti handed me the phone.

Kriti was a bit older, so she had a phone. So, Kriti said she would call me. It felt like the flowers in the garden were blooming, like the birds were singing, and I started to love the world again. I was waiting for the call from my daughters, and then finally, my phone rang. After so many years, I was hearing my daughters' voices. My whole body felt a shiver. I couldn't even speak when I heard Kriti say, "Mom." Tears filled my eyes, and after that, I couldn't stop talking to my daughters. Then Kriti said, "Mom, I will call you every day." The next day, she said, "I want to talk to Rukmini." I was not aware of what was happening, but Kriti said, "Mom, I will call you." Rukmini was so young when they took her, and she was talking to me every day now.

Kriti said, "Mom, send me your picture." And I understood because they were so young when they were taken away, so they didn't remember my face. I sacrificed everything for them, and despite all the pain they gave me, I stayed strong for my daughters. Even after the divorce, I still sent them my picture. They sent me theirs, but it didn't feel real to me. My daughters, who were as beautiful as flowers, had grown up so much. Then what? My daughters had questions. My Sita didn't even know who her mom was. My Kriti and Rukmini told me that Sita knew who her mom was. When I asked, my daughter said, "Here, dad has married someone else." Then everyone started putting pressure on my daughters, saying that they should not call anyone mom. But I knew who their mom was, so I was never ready to say anything. Even Rukmini told Sita that she didn't know where mom was. But yes, when I went to the Swaminarayan temple, I was praying to meet my daughters. The flowers in the garden were in full bloom when I met them.

Even though my daughters and I exchanged pictures, my wedding album was destroyed. Kriti, Rukmini, and Sita didn't know who their mom was or how she looked. They brainwashed my daughters and turned them against me to hide their guilt. They portrayed me as a prostitute, and they did it because they said that the credit helped me. I didn't even know which world they lived in. When someone talked to me, they would speak so badly and portray me in such a bad light. I was always open with people, and I've always had friends from school and college. When Kriti asked me, I told her everything about how her dad treated me, but I also taught my daughters never to hate their dad because he is their dad. Sita didn't know anything. She was completely unaware, but Kriti knew. My daughter told me that Kriti knew who her mom was.

Whenever I would go somewhere, they would complain and take pictures of me. They said I was not good enough. Once, when I told Kangna to take a picture, she got angry with me as if I had done something wrong by simply asking for a picture. I couldn't say anything. She argued with me and used abusive language, but no one else said anything. Once, it went too far when everyone was eating pizza. I was very tired, and my tooth was aching. I was on antibiotics. I used to cook three times a day, go out with them, do all the household work, and even cry, but still, I wasn't appreciated. Kangna had a headache, so I told her to take medicine. I was about to die, but no one noticed her food. She just wanted to eat khichdi, so I said, "You don't value pizza because of her," and then I said, "Kangna, please heat up my pizza." I wasn't even ready to eat the poison she made. I was just waiting for them to leave so I could tell her that she had no right to come to my house, nor to stay in it. What kind of compulsion was this? He had his place, yet he came to my house, and I couldn't say anything. On top of that, he would bully me, and everyone would say that Rupa was useless, that Rupa doesn't know how to say anything. That was when I realized his true nature.

One day, Kangna invited me to her house on Diwali. I got ready to go to Delhi, and we left for a day. There, I met Gurpal. He met us warmly, and even your brother was there. Something seemed off; there was tension. Gurpal was a scientist and his job kept changing, so he asked me to visit him at home. But when I reached his house, he said he had a surprise for his mom and asked me not to tell anyone. I agreed, and then we went there. We talked and had a good time. Later, Gurpal's mother said it had been a long time since she had seen me, so we chatted. Gurpal's mother asked me to stay the night, but I said I couldn't as I was staying with a friend at Kangna's place. But eventually, I stayed for a night and left the next day.

Later, they came over to my place, and after they left, I was filled with anger. I told my ex that he was no longer allowed in my house, that I didn't want to see his face there anymore, and that he wouldn't be able to do anything to my daughters either. My daughters would stay with me now. He knew that if I said something, there would be a problem because we had lived together for eight years after our wedding. He must have known a little about me. As my daughters grew older, they studied hard, and I was at peace knowing that even if their father had property, I had made my contributions. He had never really done anything, so my daughters got everything they needed, and I was at peace. They helped with their studies and made sure they had everything. They passed through college, and everything went well. We were happy. My life is my daughters; they are my world, my love.

My three daughters finished their studies and went to college. One day, Kriti told me, "Mom, I have a boyfriend who is Mexican, so talk to daddy." I knew my ex-husband would never agree because he was very stubborn and had a terrible mentality. I told my daughter that I have no problem as long as she is happy with him. Kriti's boyfriend is Costa Rican, and he is a very nice guy, and I had no problem with it. As time passed, I spoke to her daddy and said Kriti has a Costa Rican boyfriend and wants to marry him. At first, my ex-husband refused, but since I was with all three daughters, he had no choice. Eventually, my ex-husband agreed, and Kriti got married. She was very happy with him, and even now, she is very happy. Some time ago, Kriti became pregnant, and I organized her baby shower very nicely. My ex-husband and his family didn't like it at all, but I didn't care because the person my mom chose for me was not my choice. My life had already gone downhill, but I didn't want to ruin my three daughters' lives. When my three daughters were born, I decided that whatever happened to me, I wouldn't let it happen to my daughters. I would let my daughters marry whoever they wanted, even if I had to fight the whole world. I would stand for my daughters no matter who the person was, even if it was not my daughter's daddy. I didn't care about anyone; my three daughters were what mattered most to me.

My third daughter, Sita, doesn't want to get married, but she is happy in her life, so I have no problem with it. Yes, she is still young, so she might change her decision in the future, but even if she doesn't, I have no problem because I know that forcing someone to marry is not good. All Indian parents should not emotionally blackmail their children because life should be lived by the children in their own way. I know that getting married to a person I don't like is better than being married to a person who causes me stress. That's why I support my daughter, and I respect her decision. I wish Indian parents could understand that ultimately, life is for the kids to live, and we should not pressure them.

My past doesn't hold me back. They harassed me so much, to the extent that I sometimes wonder if I should just end it. But life isn't bad; it's the people in this world who are bad. Maybe this life is tied to the actions of past lives. Even if it's tough, we have to keep going. I found happiness in singing, listening to songs, talking to everyone. The world is full of both good and bad, and how we use technology is up to us. I've had my moments of romance, of flirting, of everything, and I enjoyed it all. I had to search for it because it wasn't there in my life. Yes, I did enjoy flirting, and it wasn't wrong. I liked it. I made new friends, but nothing was ever enough. To live life properly, I needed a man. My life needed that. I didn't value anything else. I needed someone to share my life with, and it's the same for everyone.

Then, one day, I gathered the courage to open my own hotel. However, it ended up being a financial loss. I had to let go of the hotel because the losses were too much. My brother never asked me for money; he just told me that whatever we do together, we will share the profit and the loss. I was relieved of my worries. My daughters were growing up, studying, and going to college. They rented their apartments and found jobs. I no longer had any worries for my daughters. After I let go of the hotel, I started wondering what I should do next. But then I realized that my life is my own now, and I need to live it for myself. My brother Ganesha, who was like a brother to me, helped me. I called him and told him I needed a job because I couldn't handle things anymore on my own. I had done everything I could, but now I was exhausted and falling into depression. Ganesh told me to come to his place. I stayed with Ganesha, and he helped me out of my depression. Today, if I'm alive, it's because of Ganesha. Otherwise, I wouldn't know if I'd still be alive in this world.

Ganesh helped me get a job through a friend of his. That was a new chapter in my life. I didn't want to go, but because of my depression, I stayed with Ganesh and eventually found a job. It was a new beginning for me. The job started at 6:00 AM and ended at 6:00 PM, with no break in between. Slowly, I reduced my working hours because the starting period was tough. I was working alone, taking care of everything. The owner lived in California and trusted me completely, so I worked hard, managing everything.

I met someone named Patty. She was like a sister to me. I started working with her and eventually hired her younger sister Billie because she also needed a job. I bought a new black Honda CR-V. I started going out, having fun, and working hard. We used to hang out, go shopping, and enjoy life. We were a great group. There was a truck driver, who was very handsome, and we used to flirt. We would go to nightclubs, dance, and have fun.

I and my friend Patty had a lot of fun together. I went to Mexico for the first time in my life with Patty, where her little sister had an apartment. The name of the town was Nogales in Mexico, and we drove there. I think it was about two hours away from Arizona. When I first went to Mexico and saw that town, it reminded me of India; all the dogs would run around there. Life was like that in India too, but now India has advanced a lot. However, in some of the earlier villages, life was just like that, and I saw exactly that in Mexico. We had a lot of fun; we went for three days.

After returning to Arizona, as usual, I got busy with work, and almost every time Patty and I would order food from the Indian restaurant. Patty and her sister had never tried Indian food in their lives before. For the first time, they had Indian food with me, and Patty liked it a lot. Every weekend, she would order Indian food with me, and sometimes we would even go to the restaurant when we had time.

There was another hotel nearby where a lady named Erika worked. I didn't know what was up with Erika; she was always jealous of me. She absolutely didn't like the way I dressed, and everyone told me I looked beautiful, which she didn't like. At another hotel, there was Manuel, the general manager, and I developed a very good friendship with him. Manuel would always come to meet me at the hotel where I worked; our three hotels were next to each other, and Erika didn't like that at all. That's why Erika was always jealous of me. Not only that, she didn't like Patty either; she didn't like that Patty and I always went everywhere together. I had no idea why anyone wouldn't like our friendship.

At the airport, Peti came to pick me up, and she really likes English chocolate, so I brought her a lot of it. After that, I went to Ganesh's house. I had to go to Yesh's place, so I called him when I got there. Peti and I didn't like him at all, but I had to come here. Manuel took us both out to eat at a restaurant, and Peti and I were very upset because I had to go to Texas. Yes, and there was no choice but to go to Texas.

One day, I received a friend request on Instagram from someone named Roy Chaudhary. I had ignored it for a long time, but then one day, as I was about to delete it, I paused and accepted it. We started liking each other's stories, and one day, we said "hi" to each other. We started talking, shared our numbers, and continued chatting on WhatsApp. He told me that he had fallen in love with my profile picture. To be honest, I liked him a lot. He was handsome and tall, the kind of guy any woman would dream of. He talked to me sweetly, saying that his heart was now with my profile picture. His way of talking and his charm won me over. It was like a dream come true. He was 12 years younger than me, but I fell in love with his nature. I felt like all the colors of life had suddenly come into my life, as if I was living in a beautiful rainbow.

Life became so beautiful, like a blossoming flower. Roy's words made me feel things I had never felt before. For the first time in my life, I felt true love, and I found what I had been searching for. After that, we would talk day and night. He was in India, and I was in the U.S.A...

Ram was very kind. Ram once told me, "If this is not meant for you, then don't do it." I told him that I would never do it. Then, he told me, "Now it's time to leave this town." My friend, Yash, lives in Texas, so now it's time to send [me] there.

And to tell you the truth, I had to do this, even though I didn't like it here at all. But I had no choice. I told him that it was a hard decision for me, and I had to do what was necessary. Then I went there. I talked to Yash, and he sent me a ticket. I went to meet him in Texas. I talked to him, and he asked me when I would be coming back. I told him that I had to go to India in August. If it's not an issue for you, I will take this job, otherwise, I will go to India and then return to work with you. Yash was very understanding and agreed immediately. He told me he had no problem with it, and I could come here in July and then go to India in August. I had to go to India for a month to meet Roy. Roy was very happy that we would meet again. I was excited too. But at the same time, his mom's health was deteriorating, which was also a concern in our lives. Because I knew his mom loved him dearly.

Later, I went to Yash's hotel on June 20 and started working there. Here, I met Tracey, who is a very straightforward girl, and I continued working at Yash's hotel. Time passed, and when it was time for me to go to India in August, during those two months, Roy was very upset because of his mom. He also started getting angry at me. We even had some arguments, but they were very loving arguments. We also had to come to terms with certain things.

To be honest, after meeting Yash and his wife Diya, I felt that there are good people like Yash and Diya in this world. Because, until then, everyone I had met had been bad, and all had taken advantage of me in some way. But Yash and Diya treated me like family. If anyone was my family, it was my three daughters, Yash, Diya, Ram, and Roy. It's difficult to forget how they stood by me through everything.

Then one day, Patsy called from Tucson, crying that her husband was treating her badly, which wasn't surprising. I told her that if she wanted to come with me, I would talk to my owner. She agreed. Then I talked to Yash, who sent her a ticket as well. She came here in July, and I was supposed to go to India in early August. It was all new to her, the idea that I would come here and then leave for India. But I assured her that Tracey, Yash, and Diya are very good people, and there wouldn't be any problems.

Everything was settled. Tickets were booked, and on the 27th of the month, I got the news that Roy's mom had passed away. I had to stay strong because there was no other option. If I had broken down, who would have taken care of Roy? And I was supposed to leave anyway. So I decided that I would go to India, and when I return, Roy would feel better. My ticket was not going to get canceled, and I had to go. We were both very happy, yet at the same time, there was fear because I knew how he would react.

I was very happy to meet Roy in India. Diya came to drop me off at the airport, and my brother had booked my ticket. During that time, my brother and mom were all going to India. Diya dropped me off at the airport. I knew my flight from Dubai would take 12 hours, but I was so happy to meet Roy that I didn't get a minute of sleep from DFW airport until I reached Dubai. I was so happy to meet Roy. My flight was 14 hours from the USA to Dubai, and then from Dubai to India, Ahmedabad.

When I reached Dubai, I was so happy that only two hours were left to reach Ahmedabad, but the flight from Dubai to India was almost on hold for 12 hours, and I was really tired.

But that happiness was something different because I was going to meet Roy, so what did 12 hours matter? I had to wait at the airport, but I didn't have any problems there. The only thing was that I didn't feel like eating anything, and yes, I had a coffee. I wandered around all the duty shops at the Dubai airport, spending the 12 hours there. I noticed a man looking at me, but I didn't pay much attention; he was Indian.

Then he casually kept looking at me. The flight from the USA to Dubai was almost 14 hours, and I didn't sleep on the flight because I was happy to meet Roy. So I sat with a coffee in one chair, having some coffee and resting a bit. The man came and sat with me, talking on the phone in Gujarati, so I felt he was Gujarati.

After finishing his phone call, he said hi to me, and I replied. Then he asked me if I was Gujarati. I said yes, and he mentioned that he had seen me before. I didn't say anything, but I thought I had seen him too. He said that he has a village in India nearby, and his name was Mukesh. He said he studied in high school in your village. His father knew mine. My dad built the high school in India where he studied. I don't know, but maybe he saw me when I went to India. He was exactly my age. Then, the 12-hour wait passed very easily. We chatted, and he knew my mom, so while talking, I didn't even realize how quickly the 12 hours went by. After that, we got sandwiches from a sandwich store; we were both vegetarians, so we ate and then did some shopping for things like perfume.

When I reached India, I became ill and couldn't leave the house for 22 days because of various issues typical of being in India. As an Indian, I knew that everyone has their own rituals and practices, and these were different too. So for 22 days, I couldn't leave the house. I left on the first of August, but our days went by like this. He was very sad, but at the same time, happy that I was going to meet him because he didn't have anyone else to talk to but me. We were very close and loved each other dearly. Then the time came when he was supposed to come to meet me, but he could only come for four days. So he came to pick me up, and we stayed in a hotel. Then, he also came to drop me off at the airport. He loved me very much.

I had to return to Anant Bhai's house, which I did not like at all. There was no proper arrangement for food. When Roy came to pick me up, Anant Bhai… O.M.G., what can I say? I was so happy that he came. I didn't want to leave. I always wished he would come back and meet him. I knew he was very sad because of his mom.

When would I meet Roy? When would I hug him? Because the first time, he came to Gujarat, and he didn't know how to get there, so after taking a taxi, the driver took him somewhere else. He was supposed to arrive at 8:00 AM but reached home at 9:30.

Then I told him, "I will come to meet you at Mein Road."

In excitement, I brought lots of food from outside, thinking he would be hungry when he arrived, and I knew he would be. But there was also fear because I wasn't sure what was in store for us. We used to talk on the phone, but this time, the trip was very bad. I was sick, my sister-in-law was sick, and the atmosphere at home was not good. It was very humid and hot.

My mom was there, so I stayed, but my sister-in-law's mom had a very bad temper. My sister-in-law didn't take care of her work at all. My sister-in-law would say that my mom was always like that, but what can be done? The day Roy arrived from Ahmedabad Airport, he took a taxi home, and just a bit later, I started feeling relieved. He was finally here. As the time to meet him got closer, my heart started beating faster.

When will he come? When will I hug him? I just wanted to see his sad face, and I didn't know how I would react. What would I say to him because, after losing his mom, I knew we would meet, but we didn't have much time. Since my sister-in-law's mom told me that the taxi driver took him somewhere else, I thought, let's go on Mein Road and keep going.

Then I heard a voice. My heart skipped a beat when I saw him. I ran to hug him. We stopped the taxi and said, "If you have to go back, come back in an hour." Then we went home together, sat down together, and he lay down next to me.

I cannot explain that feeling. It's just something different that cannot be described. It felt like I had everything I ever wanted. I felt like I was in heaven. After drinking water, he hugged me, and I felt like I was flying in the sky. It made me feel that no one in this world was luckier than me. I was so happy. That house felt like a jail, especially after my mom and sister-in-law left for England. After that, there was no tea or breakfast, nothing.

We didn't stay in that house for even five minutes after having tea and breakfast. We left as soon as we could. After that, it was just me and Roy in the car, enjoying ourselves, talking, holding hands, and hugging each other. We reached Ahmedabad, and it was 12:00 PM. We got a room at a hotel, freshened up, and were so happy. I knew that as soon as we entered the room, Roy would start crying because he had been holding back his tears. Then he hugged me tightly and cried a lot. He even let me cry too because I knew it was the end. We met after 22 days. Our plan was different, but death is in God's hands. I had to leave on August 1, but it happened on July 27. Because we couldn't leave the house for 22 days, I was waiting for him to come so we could leave together. When we finally got to be alone in our room, I was flying high, feeling like I had everything I wanted. The next morning, I got up and took him to the airport. When we got there, he was still crying because he knew it was time to say goodbye. We had met after 22 days, and even though our plan was different, God's plan is the final one.

Patsy told me that if I go to Roy, she would never speak to me again in her life, and she was right. It was a harsh truth, but it hurt. The talks between us had continued, but the distance in the relationship had grown a lot. I knew I had noticed it. For the last few times, Roy wasn't treating me nicely. If I said anything, he would get angry, and his attitude had changed. He had become very different, and whenever I would ask him about it, he would say it wasn't because of his mom. But I knew it wasn't just because of his mom. I was sure that someone else had come into his life. Even on Instagram, he was always active, but he never talked to me anymore. He didn't want the relationship anymore. If someone doesn't care about your tears, then how does it matter whether you exist or not? When someone doesn't care about your existence, why would it matter if you are there or not?

I was like a living corpse, with no interest from anyone, but working was still necessary. If I didn't work, I would have nothing. I was ready to work, but the will to live had disappeared. My brother went to India, and Ganesh told me that there were no good vibes for Roy. He said there was no need for me to go there. Ganesh was my mentor who always motivated me, and it was because of him that I wrote this book.

I was broken. What Roy did to me, my mother said that if I came to England, it would be better. I was ready to go to England. A mother is a mother; there's no one like a mother in the world. My mom helped me a lot, paying off all my debts. In our Indian culture, after God, a mother holds the highest place. My mom is worshipped by me. If she had been the person who didn't want me to marry, my life might have been different. But even then, I couldn't change what was destined.

When I told Yash that I wanted to go to England, he said okay, go. There was no problem. In other places, I had to ask the boss, who could say yes or no, but here, there was no one else. I went to England, and my brother and sister-in-law took care of me. My sister-in-law was very kind, and I met my friends and cousins there. I made many friends, but I still missed Roy. People in the world say and do things, but my passion was lost. It turned out that the love I had was fake because fake love comes with attitude, ego, costly gifts, disrespect, and lack of time. These are signs of a packaged love. Real love would have cared for me, respected me, and given time. No matter how busy you are, you should give time to your loved one.

I began to love myself and enjoy my job in England at my mom's place. I lived well, not doing much but enjoying myself. I didn't want to cause my mom any pain, so I stayed happy. When I reached England, I called Ganesh the next day to inform him, but he didn't answer. When I spoke to Sheenaben, she told me that my brother was no longer in this world. The ground seemed to disappear from under my feet. I began questioning God about why my life was like this. My mom said that if life is like this today, why did it come to this? I don't know how much I had to see in my life. I was very tired of this life.

Ganesh used to motivate and explain things to me. He would say, 'Enjoy life, don't worry.' I regretted that Ganesh was no longer in this world, and I regretted not being able to meet him. I tried to join a Zoom call with him but couldn't connect, and there were always problems. I felt like the only one welcoming me was life itself, with endless problems and Roy still lingering in my mind. There was no real person in this world except my mother. People only care about money and respect, and no one values a person. Selfishness is always present, and love is just a time pass for them. True love matters, and those who care about it make a difference. When someone is deeply hurt and cries out to God, it's true that God listens to a broken heart. I would often ask, 'What was my mistake? Where did I go wrong in loving you, respecting you, or caring for you? I fulfilled all your desires. I never bought anything for myself, but I did everything for you.' I genuinely miss him a lot, but it doesn't matter to him. The truth is, I could never see him again, not ever.

In England, while staying at my mom's place, I received a message from him saying that he needed my help, but I didn't respond because there was no longer any need to go back. The day came when I had to return from London. Diya and Myra, Diya's daughter, came to pick me up from the airport. I felt sad because Ganesh was no longer in this world, and everything in my life had turned upside down because of Roy. Also, I had to leave my mom and come here.

In the U.S., I had no family—no one except my mom. However, my small family consisted of Yash, Diya, Patsy, and the station staff. My daughters were far away, but here all the housekeepers were very nice and loving. They would often tell me that I was very beautiful and sexy, and that I deserved someone better than him. Yash would ask me every day if I was okay and would bring takeout for me throughout the week. The housekeeper would also bring lunch in the afternoon, and we would all eat together, joke around, and have fun. Tracey always looked after me and knew that sometimes I had to work at night in emergencies, but she kept an eye on me.

Despite all this, I didn't know how I could get out of my situation. Yes, our love had lasted six years, and everyone valued love, but now everything was self-centered. When I went to my mom's place, I still felt very lonely. In Indian culture, women are often seen as strong, but sometimes they are made to feel weak. Yet, when a woman decides to do something, she can accomplish it, and this strength should not be underestimated.

Often, when I was alone, I used to think and laugh about how, as a woman, I had asked him about marriage, and he had refused, saying he wasn't ready for it. Over time, his behavior had changed, becoming angrier and distant. If I wanted to ask something or make a call, he wouldn't answer. In India, while I was in the U.S., we could have made things work, but he was emotionally unavailable and self-centered.

Love, as I realized, requires effort and care. Even though I thought I wanted to help him and give everything I had, the truth was that true love should be reciprocal. It became clear that work was where I felt valued and appreciated. Myra, Diya's daughter, who was in college, used to visit during vacations. She was a sweet little girl, and seeing her always reminded me of my own daughter. Everything seemed to be pre-written by God, but friendship is one relationship that you can choose and build yourself, unlike family ties, which are preordained.

Today marks a year since our relationship ended. After working hard and coming back to my room, I often felt like I was living a film of pain. Living in this world is not easy—it's very hard. But the grace that Roy had shown me has given rise to a new beginning. My mother, who is now 75, worries about me, particularly about my marriage. I told her that if she had not forced me into it, my life might have been different. But she is my mother, and I didn't want to blame her.

Now, I pray for someone to come into my life who will care for me, love me, and take care of me. I've stopped trying to find that and have focused on loving myself and my job. I've found great happiness in writing my book. There are many women like me in the world who endure much in both Indian culture and the U.S. Many Indian women still live in difficult circumstances due to societal expectations and endure hardships. I'm grateful to God for helping me escape that situation and build a new life here.

My mother has come to understand that divorce isn't a huge crime, as it's often viewed in Indian culture. My sister-in-law's thoughts are very positive and open-minded, which has helped change my mother's perspective.

In my life, I will never forget Yash, Diya, of course Ganesh, and Sheenaben. My life is what it is because of Yash and Ganesh. All the credit goes to Yash and Diya because of them, I am very happy today. I cried as much as I could over the taxes here, I endured as much as I could, and now I have stopped. A person can cry and cry, but there comes a time when even tears dry up. My tears have dried up too.

No matter how much you do for everyone in this world, the world is not as good as you think. Now I even started to feel bad for Roy. It was good at the time, but yes, I have a desire to set an example for that woman from India, who, coming here, cannot live her life without her husband's approval. She does not find peace in that. Especially for Indian women, the values given to me have made it impossible for them to escape. But it is wrong; you do not need anyone to live your life. The world is both bad and good. I have been good to good people and bad to bad people. Those who needed me, recognized me as much as I needed them. As long as you do good for someone, that person will seem good to you. For example, Yash did so much for all the employees here, so it always felt good. Yash was truly like a boss, and there is no one like Yash. Even though all the employees are prevalent, they never missed taking advantage. I did not like it at all because Yash treated me like family. If anything went wrong, I felt it should not have happened.

Yash knew my mindset, so today he told me to go out and drink with Patsy. We decided and said to put the dinner expenses on the business card. Patsy and I went to a Mexican restaurant where we drank margaritas and then, oh my God, I got totally drunk. After that, I called Yash from the restaurant. Yash said he would come to pick us up. Patsy had also drunk but wasn't as high as I was. I got completely drunk and called Yash to come pick us up. Yash came to pick us up, and we waited outside. I was so out of it that Patsy had to help me into the car. The next day, Patsy told me all about it, how I was very drunk and started crying in the car. I told Patsy that I had scolded Roy a lot and told him, "I told you to go to the room," but I said, "No, I am staying in my room."

Yash took care of everything, making sure that the other employees didn't find out about what happened. I was completely unaware because I was so out of it. Stace arranged for a wheelchair, and she wheeled me up in the elevator to my room. I had no idea what was happening, and I ended up vomiting in the bathroom and fell asleep there for a while. When I finally made it to the bed, I didn't know how I got there. The next morning, Patsy came to wake me up. Yash had already instructed Stace and Patsy to take care of me and check if I was okay. Only a father could care for his daughter like that, and Yash took such good care of me. The next day, when I woke up and freshened up, Patsy and Stace told me that I had been completely out of it. They said, "Oh my God, you were so out of it that we couldn't even wake you." Such caring people came into my life to look after me, and I had tears in my eyes.

The next day, Yash ordered pizza for us, and we had lunch together with both girls, who were very cheerful. I had never been so drunk in my life, but in a way, it was good because everything that was in my mind came out, and I felt completely relieved. Thanks to Yash, no amount of thank you seems enough for what he has done for me. The word "thank you" seems too small for what he has done for me. Even if I were to live another seven lifetimes, I wouldn't be able to repay the debt I owe him.

Ganesh is indeed your brother, and everyone who has done good for me – my mom now understands that she made a mistake by forcing me to marry, but nothing can be done about it now. She told me that my life is mine to live as I wish, and she was happy. Every day, I receive calls from her at three in the morning, U.S. time. She still worries, but she wants me to be settled first. She says that even if she were to die, she wouldn't worry as long as I am happy.

I have started focusing on my own happiness. My book, "Ben," is our first book, and my brother Ganesh is no longer in this world. I deeply regret that he isn't here to see it. He motivated me to fulfill my dreams, and although they weren't achieved earlier, I am now determined to make my dreams come true.

There is power in determination, and I will make something of it. Even if others think negatively, I will achieve something that will eventually be appreciated. I need to show that I am doing this for myself. I want to be happy, to fly like a butterfly. I still have a lot of childhood in me, and perhaps that is why I live today with a child-like spirit. A child can be happy with a little care, and I am like that – a small child who is very happy with even a little kindness. My God is with me and will help me in everything I do. When God removes someone from our lives, we may not understand, but He has heard everything we haven't. Even anger comes to Him because He is our real parent. God makes the impossible possible, and He knows well what is best for us. God knows how to make things work out even when they seem impossible. My life in Texas has changed. I wasn't supposed to come here, but God brought me here because He knew this is where my life was meant to be. He made the situation such that I had to come here. If I hadn't come here, I wouldn't have met Stace, Yash, Diya, or Myra. I had to change my life here. I have enjoyed working and having fun. Today marks three years since I came here, and I don't even know where the time went.

I knew Roy had already made up his mind to leave me, and that time had come. I didn't force him to stay because if he wanted to be with someone else, then he should go. God is always watching. At that time, I had to go to California because my Sita was sick, and I was feeling very upset because of Roy. So, I went to California for just a couple of days to see my Sita and my friend Bulbul. Ganesh was also there, as he was going to India soon. I was happy and determined to meet him, but when Roy ended our relationship, I was in a state of shock. I canceled the ticket, and I didn't get any refund because it was a non-refundable ticket. I never thought in my life that this would happen to me.

I didn't know what life was going to do next or where it was going to take me. When you put so much weight on a bird's wings, it can never fly. That's what my ex-husband did to me, so I could neither fly nor do anything. Roy cut my wings completely, so I couldn't live or die. But even then, he continued to act nice to me. I felt like he had a problem, so I let him go. I didn't have any feelings left at that time. It was just a way to get by. When I said "not now," his attitude changed again. Then, I realized that this relationship was over, and even if you try to fix a broken mirror, the crack will always remain visible. Yes, I would smile with him as a friend and talk, but inside, my feelings had died because he had killed them a long time ago.

I knew this relationship wasn't going anywhere anymore. So, I told him, "It's time to close this chapter." But he would still continue to message me. I told him that I had bent over backwards to save the relationship, but he took me for granted and saw me as a fool. When I went to India, I took big bags with me, and I looked fine. But what he did to me was not in my mind at all. Yes, I took gifts for him because I loved him, but what he did wasn't good at all. Maybe it was good for him, but when someone who loves you so much can't even care about your tears, what's the point? And if someone is really in love, they would care for you, respect you, and make time for you, even if they are busy. That's real love.

If my best friends hadn't been there for me, Yash, Diya, and my mom, I wouldn't have survived this. My friends saw that I had gone through a hard time, and I was angry with God. What sin had I committed? I had always thought good thoughts and done good things for everyone. So, why did this happen to me? And what about me? Now, I must love myself, respect myself, and move forward.

When you think about it, your tears shouldn't have to flow for someone who doesn't deserve them. And a person who doesn't care about your feelings isn't worth your time. Yes, it hurt that I was older than him, but how was that my fault? I loved him genuinely, so I never hid anything from him. I wondered if this was really love. Maybe it was just a time pass for him. But for me, it was real love, and that's what hurt the most.

When I reached England, I realized my brother Ganesh had passed away. That took away the ground beneath my feet. It felt like life was testing me with one tragedy after another. When Ganesh was alive, he would always motivate me and tell me to enjoy life and not worry. But after his passing, I couldn't come out of the shock. It felt like my brother had left me in this world alone to face everything. My anger was towards God because I didn't understand what I had done wrong. I had always thought good thoughts and done good things, so why did this happen to me?

People talk about love, but I didn't see any real love in this world. My best friend Yash told me, "Go to England, don't worry about anything else." So, I went to England. There, I met my brother's family. My sister-in-law was very nice, and I didn't have to worry about anything. I also met my friends, my cousin sister, and my aunt. We talked a lot, and even though Roy was still on my mind, I tried to enjoy my time there. But when I realized that all of this was just a fake love, I decided to love myself.

Now, I have to think and take care of myself. Life goes on, no matter what. My life will also move forward. Everyone has a hard time, but life continues. Yes, it hurts, but we have to get back up and keep going. There is no use in forcing someone to stay in your life. If they don't want to stay, it's better to let them go. My life won't stop for anyone. If someone doesn't want to be with me, that's their decision, and I respect that. But I'll never lose hope, and I'll never give up. I'll keep moving forward.

Life is full of ups and downs, but we must learn to love ourselves first. That's the only way to survive. If we love ourselves and respect ourselves, no one can take that away from us. Life goes on, and we must move forward with it.

But it is God who makes the impossible possible. He knows what is not good for you and what wasn't meant for you, better than anyone else. Yes, life brought me to Texas, though I didn't want to come here initially. But God brought me here because He knew my life was meant to be here. Initially, I didn't want to come, but God forced me to come here. Circumstances arose that made me come here, and to be honest, after coming here, I'm happy.

If I hadn't come here, I wouldn't have met Stace, Yash, Diya, or Myra. Coming here, even though I was unhappy, was necessary for a change in my life. Even though I loved having fun and working every day, my life had changed after coming here. It's been three years since I came here, and those three years have gone by so quickly. The world has changed; I have endured so much, gone through so many difficult situations, but yes, my inner self, my soul, tells me to wake up and be strong. I was strong before, and I am still strong, and I will always be strong. Awaken the strong Rupa inside you and recognize who you are in this world.

Every woman in this world, if she wants, can do anything. God has placed that power within her. At one point, I was broken, but I didn't let love make me that weak. Yes, I focused, I started writing my book. After writing half of it, I stopped, but then I decided that no, Rupa, the time has come to finish the book. This is my book, remember the days, the hardships you faced; they will become your strength, your inspiration to become something, and you will achieve your dreams. Keep your spirit alive, and to be honest, a strength has come within me that makes me determined to become something.

All I want is my mom is here, so I feel that once I am settled, she won't worry about death. That's all she wants—to see me accomplish something in life. I feel a deep regret that my brother Ganesh, who was a part of our first book, is no longer in this world to witness it. He was the one who motivated me. The dreams that I couldn't fulfill before, I will now definitely achieve. You should have strength within you, and I will become something. Rupa, who was once disliked by everyone and made to feel bad, will one day be admired by all for what she has achieved. I don't need to do anything to prove myself to anyone, I just need to do it for myself. I want to live my life happily as it is, to fly like a bird and flutter like a butterfly. There is still a lot of childhood innocence in me, and I am like a little child. Maybe that's the reason I am still alive today. Like a child who stops crying when given something they want, I am a child who gets happy when someone speaks kindly to me or does something nice. I get so happy, and there's no limit to it. My God is with me, and He will help me in whatever I do.

When God removes someone from your life, we don't understand at the time, but He has heard everything that we haven't. The anger we feel is also directed at Him because He is our real parent. But God is the one who makes the impossible possible. He knows what isn't good for us, what isn't meant for us, better than anyone else. Yes, my life changed in Texas. I didn't want to come here at first, but God brought me here because He knew my life was meant to be here. Initially, I resisted, but God forced me here, creating situations that made me come. And honestly, now that I'm here, I'm happy. If I hadn't come here, I wouldn't have met Stace, Yash, Diya, or Myra. Coming here has changed everything, even Patsy's life.

It's been three years since I came here, and I don't even know where the time went. The world changed around me, and I endured so much. I faced situations that were beyond my control. But my inner spirit says, 'Rupa, wake up! Awaken the Rupa within you!' You are a strong woman—you were before, and you still are, and you always will be. Recognize that strong Rupa within you. Know who you are. In this world, not just you, but every woman can achieve anything if she chooses to. God has given us that strength. I, too, was once a businesswoman. Love can't make you that weak. Then I focused, and I decided that the time had come to finish the book I had left halfway through.

Now is the time, Rupa. The days when you faced hardships will become your strength, and they will inspire you to become something. You have to become something, and you will. Keep your spirit alive. Honestly, a new strength has risen within me. I have decided that I am going to become something, and I will.

Don't stop until you reach your destination, and don't give up on your dreams. Yes, today, I am working on myself, and this is a new birth of Rupa. I have forgiven everyone who wronged me, including Roy. God knows their actions and deeds, and I have no problem with anyone. Today, I am forgiving everyone and moving forward. They needed me, but I will live for those who truly love me—family, friends. Life doesn't stop for anyone, and it won't stop now. I've endured all the pain and challenges I had to, and now, I have developed the courage.

Rupa will do something; Rupa will become something. Life has taught me that we must trust ourselves because in darkness, not even our shadow supports us. I have received support from everyone when I needed it the most. Now I understand that if we get everything in life, what will be left to do? It's the unfulfilled desires that make life exciting. This is life. In life, we never know when people and circumstances will change. I paid a heavy price for my relationships, but now I am free from those relationships. Just like a bird that gets free from a cage and flies in the open sky, I am also free. There was no point in holding onto relationships forcefully. Today, I am ending this book, but this is not the end. This is the new birth of Rupa. I will try to write another book, and I will definitely write it. Today, I have freed Roy from my relationships and memories. My new life has begun.

As time passed, my Kriti had a baby boy, and I was very happy. When I first held my grandson, Aryan, I felt like my Kriti had come back. His childhood was back; he looked just like my Kriti when she was little. My daughters and I were very happy when Kriti had her baby boy. I lost track of time with him. Yes, my ex-husband was also happy inside.

My grandson is very cute, and his name is Aryan. He is totally the opposite of Kriti. When she was little, she was very calm, while Aryan is a bit mischievous. I enjoyed playing with him. My second daughter, Rukmani, also had a boyfriend who is half American and half Mexican. My third daughter, Sita, doesn't want to get married ever, and I respect her decision. I never wanted to force any of my daughters to marry; I just want my three daughters to be happy, and their happiness is my happiness. I want to give them everything I never had. I don't blame my mom either because she also faced a lot of hard times. My mom grew up in India without her parents. All my mom's sisters and her brother were in England, and my mom and my aunt were left in India by my grandfather.

My mom didn't know what the love of parents is, that's why I don't blame my mom for choosing that guy whom I married.

My three daughters and I were more like friends than a mother and daughter. We never hid anything from each other. My three daughters were also very open with me. They were my friends. Whenever my daughters and I went to the mall or anywhere, everyone would tell us that we looked like four sisters. It never felt like they were my three daughters. And yes, when daughters grow up, it's necessary to have a relationship with their mom as a friendship. For me, my three daughters are my best friends with whom I share everything and never hide anything.

For me, the three daughters given to me by God were a very big gift, and I lived my life looking at them. A mom is the only person in this world who is ready to fight her entire life for her son or daughter.

I have become a grandmother not once but twice. My second granddaughter's name is Pihu, and she is very sweet. OMG, she looks just like my daughter, so sweet and cute, and she has turned two years old today.

But Patty and I didn't care about anyone else. I believe everyone should help each other; all the business people should be together, so there's no point in being jealous. But Erika didn't understand that. Manuel would always come to talk to me and would take me to the restaurant sometimes. There was one town, one street, and three hotels together, and I believed that when necessary, we should help each other. Patty and I were all in it together. Patty's life was not very good. Whenever we went to the mall, I would always buy her some gift. During that time, Patty and her husband didn't have a good relationship either. I had no idea where the time went for them with work.

To tell the truth, everyone who worked at that hotel was very nice to me. I had already become very fond of Patty. Patty's nature is very sweet. She is two years younger than me, but I always tell her that she is older than me in age, and I say that because she has a lot more maturity than I do, which I don't have. I don't want to bring that out because there's a little child in me that I never want to lose. I am childish, and Patty is just right; she understands a lot, which is why I always tell her that she is not two years younger than me, but older. There was nothing that Patty hid from me; she always told me everything about her life and what happened in her life.

In my life, I have never had a friend like Patty until now. One time, Patty said, "Let's go to Rocky Point, which is in Mexico," and I agreed. Patty, her daughter Melina, and I went to Rocky Point for a vacation, and we had a lot of fun on the beach. We stayed there for three days, and those three days were really good. Yes, I had one problem: I am a vegetarian, and there were very few choices for me to eat, but still, we enjoyed Rocky Point a lot. We stayed at a resort, and we drove there. Rocky Point was almost like a four to five-hour drive, according to my estimate, but it was a lot of fun, of course, because I didn't drive. Patty drove, and it rained a lot on the way, but Patty drove all the way to Rocky Point. For me, it was entirely new. I exchanged Mexican money; it was the first time I saw Mexican currency. After three days of enjoyment, we returned to normal and went back to work.

My brother, Ganesh, who lived in Green Valley, Arizona, I always used to go to his house, and Patty and her sister would come too. I would usually stay at their place from Friday to Saturday and come back on Sunday evening to the town where I worked. There was another hotel there where an Indian man named Jimmy worked. One day, he came to meet me at my hotel, and Patty's sister was working at the front desk. Jimmy handed her his business card and said he had come to meet me. I didn't know who he was. Patty's sister came into my office and told me that someone named Jimmy had come to meet me. I said to tell him to wait, and then I stepped out of my office. He was sitting in the lobby of my hotel, and I went and met him. I told him I didn't know him. He said he had also taken a hotel in that town. I told him, "Okay." He said we are in the same town, so if either of us needs something in business, we can talk; that's why I came here to meet you. I said, "Okay, no problem."

Then I offered him tea or coffee, and he said, "No, thank you," and we went to my office to talk. While talking, he directly asked me if I was single. I found it a bit odd that someone would ask a woman directly if she was single when meeting for business for the first time. So I asked him, "Did you come here to discuss the hotel business or to talk about my personal life?" He smiled a little and then looked at me and said, "I'm a very straightforward man."

I was angry, but I didn't say anything. Then I was told that I found out from the town that you are single and that I'm interested in you, so I came to meet you specially to talk about business, not just a casual chat. I told your desk clerk that I came here to talk business. I asked them who told you this and who is spreading all this gossip that I am single. They told me they wouldn't tell me right now who told them. I made it clear that I don't like all this gossip; just speak straight with me about who told you. No person can force any woman. This person was just someone who talked to him, and he liked me. I really felt like I could tell him to get out of here in anger.

But I needed to know who told him such things. Later, he invited me to an Indian restaurant. I said I would see, giving him Jimi's phone number, and he left. Later, I told Peti, "There's a problem with the Indian man today." Peti told me, "Please tell me who said you are single." I said I didn't know. Then I talked about this with my brother Ganesh, and the next day Jimi called me back. I told him I had no interest, neither in him nor in going to the Indian restaurant with him. Jimi spoke badly about me in town, where they played cards. It was a small town, and all the Indians went together, so Jimi talked badly about me because I refused to go to the restaurant with him, saying I had no interest. His ego was hurt, and then he started speaking badly about me to everyone. I told my brother that Jimi talks badly about me like this. Ganesh, who is known to everyone in town, has helped many people. Ganesh told me he would personally go and talk to him. I told my brother no, I didn't want any problems. Then my brother Ganesh told me, "You neither want problems nor let me say anything. Now there's only one way; you will have to leave this town." It escalated because Jimi was talking about me to the entire Indian community. Honestly, it didn't affect me. I had already risen above all this; I really didn't care what people thought or said about me. I was the kind of person who just wanted to enjoy my life. I didn't care what the world thought or what was happening around me. I already had many problems in my life.

Peti and I were both busy with our work and enjoyed ourselves. Then I hadn't met my mom for a long time, and I needed to go to England. So, I left the hotel where I was and decided to go to England. I went to England for a very short trip because I was going for only one week. I spoke with my brother Abhilash about his friend who lives in Texas. I told Ganesh that before going to Texas, I wanted to go to England to meet my mom for just a week. So, I was happy, booked the ticket, and I left for England. Peti came to drop me at the airport.

When I got to the airport, my flight got delayed, and it was a very small airport. I got bored waiting at the Arizona airport. It was a six-hour flight. While at the airport, I received a call from Yesh. I told Yesh that I was going to meet my mom in England and that I would call him back after I arrive at the airport. I was going for a week because my brother Ganesh had already spoken with him at night and given him my phone number for work. I told Yesh that I would call him. It was time for my flight, and I was very happy to be meeting my mom after a long time. My mom was so happy to see me that she said, "Why are you coming for just one week? You should come for a longer time." It had been a long time since I went to England.

When I go to my mom's house, I feel like a queen. My mom wakes me up in the morning and has tea ready for me, breakfast prepared, and whatever I want to eat for lunch and dinner is made according to my choice. Whenever I go to sleep or wake up, my mom doesn't say anything to me. She doesn't let me do any work. I went to England to stay for just a week, but I got sick because the cold there was terrible, and I had sinus issues. Where did that week go? I didn't even realize it, and then it was time to return to Arizona.

From the Dubai airport, it is a beautiful airport. I also took some pictures, and I wanted to click a picture like Roy did when he went to Dubai. So, I clicked a similar picture, and in doing that, the 12 hours went by quickly. It was time for our flight from Dubai to India, and now our destination was very close. From Dubai, it was only a two-hour flight to Ahmedabad.

I was lost in the dream of going to meet Roy, and the happiness of meeting him was very different for me. That 12-hour wait didn't feel like anything. To be honest, I didn't sleep on that long flight; I just listened to my songs and got lost in my own world. When we arrived at Ahmedabad airport, we cleared immigration and went to baggage claim.

Mukeshbhai helped me a lot in getting all my bags from the belt. As soon as we got out of the airport, his family came to pick him up. He introduced me by saying, "This is my sister; you know her." Then he said that his dad was friends with mine and that I was his daughter. He invited me to his home, but I said I would come if I had time because I was only in India for a little while, just for a month. So, if I have time, I will definitely come. We parted ways from there.

When I reached India, my brother came to pick me up because he had already reached India from England. As soon as I arrived in India, I called Roy first to tell him I was in India. I knew that his mom was no longer in this world, so he was sad about that. I knew it was necessary to tell him that I had come to India and that we were going to meet. Actually, our plan was different, but because of his mom's passing, our plan changed a bit. Earlier, I was going to go directly to Roy, and he was supposed to come to pick me up from the airport, but his mom's death changed everything, and I had to go to my family first.

33) When it was time to return from India, Roy came to drop me off at the airport after we met. To be honest, I didn't want to leave him and come back here at all, but I also had to come back here. After dropping me off, Roy went back, and I returned to Dubai, where there was a 12-hour layover. I booked a room there, stayed in a hotel room in Dubai, and then had to go back to the airport to continue my journey. I called from Dubai and spoke to Roy, who also told me that he really didn't like being here without me. He had to drop me off at the airport and was supposed to head home afterward. I told him to come and pick me up when I returned, but he said if his mother hadn't passed away, he would've come all the way to Dubai to drop me off. He said he would have come to Dubai with me and gone back to India, but everything is in God's hands. So, that didn't happen, and soon it was time for my flight. I boarded from

Dubai, and honestly, I was very tired; the 12-hour wait had taken a toll on me. When I arrived in India, I felt relieved.

Waiting for 12 hours was tough, and returning from India was even harder because Roy wasn't with me. Diya came to pick me up at the airport here in the USA. After arriving from the airport, I freshened up, and Diya made tea and a warm breakfast for me. After having that Thai breakfast, I don't even know when I fell asleep. The next morning, I woke up, sent a message saying I'd reached the USA safely, and Roy replied, "Okay, now rest; you must be very tired." I told him I wasn't tired anymore and felt refreshed after a good sleep. I also told him that I didn't like being here without him. Roy also said he didn't like being here either, but we had to come here as it was necessary. I had to call Roy to the USA, apply for his visa, and after two weeks of being here, I discussed some important papers with him that I needed for his application. One day, I asked him a question I felt was necessary, and I don't know what happened, but he got angry at me. I asked if he felt we weren't working out, then he should let me know. He said, "No, it's not that; I've just been disturbed since my mom passed, and you know that." And I did know, as he was very close to his mother.

But what happened has already happened, and now we just have to move forward. Later, Peti often told me that although she knew Roy's mother had passed, it didn't mean he could just say whatever he felt whenever he was angry. She said that wasn't right, and I agreed, saying his mind was upset, but I knew he loved me deeply. I needed some important papers from him, but he was a bit delayed in giving them to me. Days turned into months, and before I knew it, a year had passed. I got so busy with work here, working alongside Tesi and Peti. We all worked together very well, and Stacey, too, was very helpful. After coming from India, I asked Peti if she was adjusting here.

So, we made another plan. We would meet later. My brother had a car, and I went to stay at his house for a few days, and I told him I wanted to meet Roy soon. But the time that I had in India was too short. After a few days, my brother arranged a big family function. Roy was also invited to that, so I met him there. Seeing him again after so long brought a lot of happiness to my heart. He really liked me too; I could see that. He always told me, "I was waiting for you. I'm really happy you are here." He started talking to me a lot about what I had done in life, my family, and everything.

While I was in India, I received a call from Peti saying she had problems at the hotel and needed my help. I told her I'd come back to the USA soon. But there was no way to change the ticket back, and we were enjoying our family time together.

After some time, I went back to my brother's house, and we both talked together. We decided to go out for dinner. He said he would take me to a special restaurant, and then he picked me up from my brother's house. While we were out, we talked a lot and enjoyed ourselves. He told me, "I want to spend some time with you. I'll keep visiting you in the USA." I said okay, but I also told him I didn't want any complications. I made it clear to him that I didn't want any complications in my life.

After that, I went back to the USA, and I stayed for a week in my brother's house, and then we went back to Arizona. It was still cold in the USA, but it was winter there. So, I made it clear to him that I didn't want to have any complications in my life. And I think my brother Ganesh also wanted the same thing, so that's why he was happy when I was happy, and he kept encouraging me about my happiness.

After that, I returned to my place, and when I reached, Peti was waiting for me. When I returned, I was really happy to meet everyone after a long time, and I started my daily life again.

My brother who lives in England is named Amit. He always talks to me on the phone and explains things to me. My brother is a completely calm person. To be honest, my brother has a nature like my daddy, but I don't remember my daddy much. My mom used to say that my brother is just like my daddy. Both of them, along with my brother and I, support each other. I gradually started coming out of my sadness.

Time passed, and I kept working. Yes, I slowly began to move. Ganesh's daughter lives here in Texas. Ganesh's daughter came here from Canada and has bought a house here. So Ganesh called me to say that he would come to meet me, and I was very happy because I had just come out of a relationship with Roy. When I heard that Ganesh was coming here, I was very happy. Ganesh told me that I would have to come to pick him up, and both Peti and I were very happy that Ganesh was coming to meet me. On that day, Peti and I worked in the morning and then left. I told Yesh that Ganesh was coming, and Yesh welcomed Ganesh very well. It was almost an hour's drive from here for me and Peti, and we must have left around 10.

When we got there, as always, Surabhiben made a very nice lunch. Peti was very excited because he always came with me to Ganesh's house in Arizona, so he knew that Surabhiben was an expert in cooking. We had lunch, and her daughter also welcomed us very well. After lunch, we sat and talked for a while, which was very enjoyable. After that, we left. Before that, Yesh asked me everything about what drinks Ganesh would like? What not? We brought everything for Ganesh, and Yesh and Diyaben both welcomed Ganesh very well. We sat there for a while, and then Ganesh was given a room. It was a hotel, obviously, so it was Ganesh's habit to rest for a bit after lunch in the afternoon. He went to the room to relax, and I and Surabhiben liked to go around the store, so I took Surabhiben to the store. I told Peti to also go and relax, and I took Surabhiben to the store. After wandering around the store for a long time, we came back. When we returned, Diyaben was there, and at that moment Ganesh had also woken up from his sleep. So Ganesh, we sat in the office and talked for a while, and then I went out to do a little something with Ganesh. It was time for dinner. We returned, and Ganesh was talking to Yesh in the office, and I was with Surabhiben in our room.

Then Surabhiben and I went to our car, and Ganesh came with us for the night. When we went to Yesh's other house, Yesh's elder brother and sister-in-law welcomed Ganesh and Surabhiben very well and made many dishes for dinner. Both Surabhiben and I liked it very much, as the way people welcomed us was really nice, and I was also very happy. We sat there until almost 10:00 in the evening, then returned home. When we came home, Ganesh came to my room, and we talked until around midnight. I was very happy, and during that time, to be honest, I really needed Ganesh to talk about many things. Ganesh understood me very well; I didn't know how to express myself, but he would understand what I wanted to say and what I needed. He was a very good friend with whom I could openly share everything.

He explained things to me very well. I talked to him about what Roy did with me, and during that time, to be honest, talking to him was very necessary. By talking to him, I felt a lot of peace inside. I didn't know how he explained things to me, and he knew how to support my mental state. While talking to him, he told me that I should never feel guilty about anything, about why it happened or what I should have done. Nothing. When you both met, you and Roy were at the hotel enjoying yourselves. Enjoy that time. Just keep that in mind. After that, what happened or didn't happen, there's no need to think about that. At that moment, that minute, that second was meant to be enjoyed. What happened afterward was just meant to happen. Don't mess up your mind by thinking about it.

We have no control over anything. We think that all this belongs to us, that we do it, but that's all wrong. What was meant to happen in the past will happen. So don't think about that. Just think that as long as you were with him, you enjoyed it. That time was important. What happened afterward isn't worth thinking about. He explained it to me in such a way that in my mind, it all clicked that Ganesh was right. That's why I would talk to him for hours every day.

After that, after midnight, Ganesh said, "Alright, I'm going to sleep," and went to his room. The next morning, we received a call from Diyaben asking us to let her know ten minutes before Ganesh and Surabhiben woke up so that she could prepare hot tea for them. When Ganesh woke up, that day, Stacy was working at her desk, so I always talked to Ganesh about my real brother who lives in England. But even though Ganesh isn't my real brother, he was just like one.

Then I introduced Ganesh to Stacy, and Stacy always smiled; she was always happy. Her name was "Smiley Girl." I talked a bit with her, and then we went to Diyaben's place for breakfast. We talked a bit there and after breakfast, I wanted to talk with Ganesh, so he said, "Let's go for a walk at the back of the hotel; there's a very beautiful church there, and there's a nice trail for walking." We went for a walk for about half an hour, and then we went to drop Ganesh at his daughter's place. After having some tea and snacks there, we returned home, and Ganesh called me. He said that there's no need to think about what happened but to focus on what to do next. He suggested that I should go visit my mom in England for some time so that my mind would refresh a little.

A week later, he was going to leave his daughter's place to go to India. After going to India, I would always talk to Ganesh on the phone, and we both knew that I was coming out of a situation. He didn't want me to go back into depression, so he called me every day even after he went to India and talked to me. He told me that he didn't have any good feelings for Roy. I said, "Okay, it doesn't matter. What has happened has happened; now nothing can change." I got busy with work, and I didn't even have the chance to stop what I was doing.

While working a little more, some time passed. Then Ganesh returned from India to here, and after a while, I decided to go to England to meet my mom. I told Yesh that I was going to England to meet my mom and booked my ticket. After that, I told Ganesh that I was going to England, and he said, "You can't go alone." I said, "You should come with me," but he had a doctor's appointment, so he couldn't come. He always wanted to go to England with me. His relatives live there too, but he felt comfortable going with me.

I called my mom and informed her that I was coming to England, and she was very happy. I also called my brother Amit, and he was supposed to come to pick me up at the airport. This time, I was going to England for 15 days. Everyone here loves the Taco Bell sauce, so Yesh specially brought some for me to give to my mom and everyone. To be honest, my family really liked it, and the time had come for me to leave for England. Diyaben came to drop me at the airport. Before that, there is an Indian restaurant on the way, so Diyaben took me there for lunch, saying that there won't be anything to eat at the airport.

So I had lunch there, and then they dropped me off at the airport. From here to Florida, there was one stop. From Florida to England, the flight was with DFW. I felt very bored at the airport and didn't know what to do, so I just sat and ate.

Then, as the flight time approached, I told Diyaben that it was about time. I called Ganesh and talked to him. When my boarding began, the flight from Florida was about two hours. I reached Florida and then called Ganesh again to talk. I didn't even realize how the time passed; I wasn't feeling hungry.

The flight from Florida to England was around six hours. When I landed at the airport in England, I felt relieved. To be honest, boarding the flight was such a hassle; I couldn't find my bag because it was always late. After getting my bag, I called my brother. He was waiting for me at the airport. I told him to get the car to pick me up from the airport. Amit picked me up, and when we arrived home, my mom was very happy to see me.

The entire family was very happy that I was there, and they were very happy to see me. I spent time with them, and it felt like home. My mom said, "You have to take me out for dinner; it's been so long since I've been out." So we took my mom out for dinner, and they were happy to see me and the Taco Bell sauce. When I opened the box of sauces, everyone was shocked and happy.

After spending about 10 days there, it was time for me to return, but I didn't want to leave. Everyone was feeling sad, and they said I should stay for a few more days, but I had to return because my job was here. The last day was very emotional for everyone, and Amit dropped me off at the airport again. I felt bad leaving them, but they understood.

I flew back from England to Florida, and from Florida back home. I had a great time, and after returning home, I had a few things to share with Ganesh. I immediately called him, and he was very happy to hear about my trip to England and how my family was doing. After that, I got busy with work again.

At that moment, my mind was calm; I got busy in my work again, and everything was good. I felt very comfortable. I still had a lot to share with Ganesh. Even now, I talk to Ganesh and he understands everything very well. When I talk to him, my heart feels lighter, and I am grateful for everything.

One day, we decided, my sister-in-law and I, that let's take the double-decker bus, which is not here in America but can only be seen in England and Europe. I really wanted to ride in it after a long time. My sister-in-law and I always took the bus together, and that day we were going to Brighton, and the weather was also very nice. When I lived in England, the weather was very cold; you wouldn't get to see nice weather for six months. Now, since the weather was good there, my sister-in-law, both my nieces, and I went to Brighton, and we spent the whole day there. In the evening, we returned, and I enjoyed sitting at the front of the double-decker so much that I took many videos to show my friends here. We enjoyed that day a lot and then came back home.

I stayed there for three days with my three daughters because my mom had arrived in England before me to meet them. They came specifically to meet my mom, and then they stayed there for just one week after meeting her, and then they returned to America.

I was supposed to stay for 15 days, and during those 15 days, I spent time with my mom, my brother, my sister-in-law, and both my nieces. In the evenings, when I would go to my room, my nieces would come to my room with me. We would chat for a long time, late into the night.

My aunt also came to see me. My friend came to meet me and then had lunch with me one day. After that, we went to the station to drop her off because there everyone travels by train, and very few come by car. My time with my mom was very nice. She comforted me a lot and explained many things to me. Yes, my mom always understood me very well as a friend. I shared everything with her; I also talked a lot with my sister-in-law, and we would go shopping. My mom did all the shopping for me; her help was immense. If my mom hadn't helped me in my life, I don't know how I would have lived my life. Of course, I was working during the starting period, but back then, my aunt made me feel at home. I told everyone on the staff that I would bring them chocolates from England. We went to the park, and I remembered my friend with whom I always went to that park, and I don't know how it would feel when I go to that park alone after such a long time, with my one friend, the one with whom I went to college and school. Those memories were very sweet; life has everyone busy with their own work, and only sweet memories remain.

It felt good to stay with my mom; it felt like I had come back home. I also spent some time with my aunt, and I am very close to that aunt. I have five other aunts, but I am very close to this aunt, and her daughter is the one I used to drop off at school and pick up from school myself when she was young. On weekends, when I worked, she would come with me to the mall. When she came to visit me at home, everyone was together; we stayed at home because I had gone to England to meet my mom, and it felt like a celebration, as if there was a wedding; the whole family was under one roof, my three daughters, my brother's two daughters, everyone stayed together.

I didn't take anything except my clothes in my bag when I went there, and when I came back, I brought two bags with me. My mom sent me so many chocolates to show that plus other things that I had to give to my staff where I work here. I definitely won't forget my friends Patty and Stacy, and of course, Yesh and Myra, who also loved those chocolates. All the shopping was done by my mom because when she comes here, there's no worry. I didn't take any money with me to go there, so I went without any worry.

Then my time came to return here, and I didn't like it at all to leave my mom behind and come back. After such a long time, I had gone there, and when you go back home and then have to return, everyone feels the same way; I felt that way too. But this had to happen, and my mom and sister-in-law came to drop me off at the airport. My flight was also late, and it was early morning, so I was very tired. To tell the truth, waiting at the airport is the most annoying thing, and I left after breakfast; that was it. There was also no food at the airport because I am vegetarian, so I didn't like anything.

From there, I came to Florida, Tampa, and felt a little good; the flight was on time, and I had coffee at the airport. There, I met a nice lady, and time passed while talking with her. She is also here in America, and while talking with her, I lost track of time, and it was nice that she was seated next to me on the flight from Florida, so the time passed very easily.

I arrived here, took a day off, and then started working the next day. Yes, I was sad because Ganesh is no longer in this world. It felt like a pain in my heart, and I couldn't control it. Patty also knew Ganesh very well. I called Surabhi Ben and told her that I know how hard it must be for her since her husband is not in this world anymore, and they were always together, going wherever, whether in India or anywhere in America. The relationship between husband and wife is like that. There is no one in this world who has not received help from Abhilash. In my life, I will always have one regret, that I could not meet Ganesh. Yes, I only met him when he came here to meet me, and then he went to India. After going to India, he returned here, and I could not meet him, and he is no longer in this world.

I always talked with Surabhi Ben, so she felt good talking to me, and even though I cried, I explained to her that once a person goes to God, they never come back, so it's important to stay strong. I also felt sad inside, but I couldn't do anything else. I did say that you should come here and spend some time with me, but in our Indian culture, there is a tradition that after a person's death, we have many rituals to perform, so Surabhi Ben was going to India for that in October. She told me that until that is finished, she won't come to spend time with me.

I told her that once everything is done, please do come to spend some time with me after returning from India. It's been almost six months since Ganesh passed away, but it still feels like it just happened. Time is flying, and everyone has to do their work because life doesn't stop for anyone. Life may feel heavy, but we have to live it.

Yes, I miss Ganesh a lot. Whenever I needed him in my life, I would call him, and he would motivate me. Now, there is no one around.

But here, I feel good with all the girls I work with. My nature becomes like a little girl with the little girls. When my friend's daughter Myra came during the vacation, I would go out with her. She liked being with me, calling me aunt. Patty and Tessie and I went to the restaurant, and she also liked going to coffee shops or stores.

ORDER
& PAY
HERE

Then Surabhi Ben called, and she said, "Please, do you have a relative with whom you can talk on the phone? If you like, you can marry that person." I did speak with respect, but I had no interest in marrying that person Surabhi Ben talked about. It's not that easy to get out of one relationship and immediately be ready to marry someone else. But I had to listen to Surabhi Ben, so I talked to that person. However, I had no interest in marrying him, and when Ganesh was alive, he had told me that his cousin's son was not right for me. So, I didn't talk to him, and I also told Surabhi Ben that when Ganesh was around, he told me that, so the person you asked me to talk to is not right for me. I am not made for him, or he is not made for me. I need someone in my life who cares, loves, and is caring.

I don't want to get trapped in a wrong relationship again, so I told Surabhi Ben no. I did talk to that person as you suggested, but I have no interest in him, so I told her there's no problem.

I called my daughter and told her that aunt mentioned a relative of hers that she wanted me to talk to. My daughter told me, "Mom, don't forget that Dad never treated you well, and then after that, your relationship with Roy broke off." My daughter said, "Mom, I want to see you happy. Don't go back to being sad, and I will never do an arranged marriage. Wait for the right time because you have seen a lot of sadness in life. We want you to be happy; we have no problem, but take your time until the right man comes into your life." To tell the truth, my second daughter is very mature, very understanding, and has a lot of wisdom. My three daughters have no problem with anyone coming into my life, especially with Indian kids. It is a good thing that they respect and love me very much.

Now, they all understand me very well. Now, as long as I am with my daughters, I feel good, and that is enough for me. They are there to take care of me, and I feel fine. I'm also thinking that I will take my time. I don't want to rush into anything. If a good man comes into my life, that's fine, but I won't compromise. I want the best for me, and that is enough.

I have a friend named Jimmy Shah. She is so beautiful. She got married at a young age; the person she was in love with was not allowed to marry her by her mom and dad. She ended up marrying the boy that her mom and dad chose for her. They had a daughter who was only two years old, and then her husband passed away. After that, she couldn't even go to her mom and dad's house, and her husband's parents were very bad to her. They gave her so much sorrow that they didn't even ask her about anything. And Indian parents, look, in this age, they told her that now this is your home, and you have to live there. Even if the daughter is sad, she has to stay there. She has been living there for a long time.

Then I always used to talk to her, and I told her that you are still very young. I mean, my friends and I are almost the same age, but she has many desires. Since her husband is gone, she felt she couldn't live her life. Over time, she met a boy and fell in love with him; she also met him on a social site, Facebook. Then she asked me for help and told me that she had fallen in love with this boy. I said yes, you have to live your life and not care about the world.

What will they say to you? What will they think? Nobody will come to pay your bills; you do all the work yourself. After that, she decided to get married. They got married, and after a little while, that boy fell in love with someone else, and my friend got a divorce. So, I told her, "I don't know if all the girls from our village have had someone crush on them or what, but why does this happen with every girl from our village?"

My young daughter Sita fell ill and went to California. I spent some time there with my friend Balbir, who has always supported me a lot in life. She's also a single mom, and I believe that only a woman who has gone through similar challenges can truly understand another woman. I feel that someone who has already faced issues with their husband, like I did, can understand you more deeply. If anything happens to my youngest daughter Sita, I feel as if my life is slipping away because she's the youngest and my most cherished child. She has a slight problem with her leg, but I always tell her, "As long as we can walk, it doesn't matter if there's a problem. Life isn't the same for everyone; God has given us this life, and she's both strong and smart."

The friends who have helped me in life are like angels sent by God. Anyone can talk, but real friends are those who stand by you when you truly need them. While I was in California, my friend helped me a lot. Her husband was in India and had abused her as well, so she came to America and faced many hardships. She raised her sons on her own, which is why she can understand my pain. There was a time when we would sit at her house for hours talking. Her son was addicted to drugs, and she would often share all her troubles with me. She would always say that he never listens to her, and sometimes she would cry, working six days a week in an Indian salon, where, for some reason, I've observed that many Indian women seem unhappy.

I've noticed that many Indian women don't seem happy, and I wonder how they live, likely staying because of their children. Some women don't have the courage to get a divorce, so they just go along with life as it is. But why shouldn't women have the right to live their lives, their dreams, and their desires? Is that really a life worth calling life? In my village, none of the daughters received a good husband; every girl has faced some kind of problem. This happens because Indian parents don't ask their daughters and marry them off to anyone. My friend, who lives in England, and I often talk about how none of the daughters in our village seem to be happy. I don't know why, but if I'm being honest, maybe only 10 out of 100 daughters would have taken a divorce, and I'm one of them. All the other girls live their lives thinking about what society will say, even if they're not happy. I believe it's better to live alone and happily than to live a life where you suppress your emotions. But these are my thoughts, and I don't impose them on others; everyone has their own views.

I talked to my mom and told her, "Look, that's why marriage should never be forced. Arranged marriage, when parents do everything for you, but then the life is not for them to live; it is for their daughter or son to live. That's why it is good to marry someone you like." How can you marry someone you have never met or seen? Here in America, with everyone I talk to, they all say that in India, parents pick the boy or girl for your marriage. Often I feel embarrassed, but I also say that yes, that was the time, but now everything has changed; now every boy and girl marries the person they love, and that is very good and how it should be.

I am happy that I have come out of that toxic relationship with my ex-husband. Yes, I struggled a lot, but it was worth it. Living in a forced marriage is not as good as being happy on your own. It's not easy for women and single moms to live life.

I am also happy that my mom has become open-minded. I love my mom very much. My mom understands me very well in everything, and my sister-in-law is also open-minded. After struggling so much, I have become a person who does not care what the world thinks about me or what they say. I do what I want to do; I have become like that now. The world has taught me that, and all the people I met in this world who came into my life have made me who I am, and I have become that. It is also necessary in this world.

In this world, I owe three people my life: first, my mom, who brought me into this world; second, Ganesh, who brought me out of depression; and third, Yesh. I can never forget the debt to these people in my life.

Now I have learned to live my life for myself, not to impress people because this world is such that when we leave this world, nobody will remember us by our name, but yes, they will know us as a body. That's why I have spent my time impressing my own life. Now, when I spend money, I do it for the things I like. I love to laugh, so I laugh so much sometimes that my stomach hurts. I also love to dance, whether I dance well or not, but my heart becomes happy. But now I am living for my own happiness because dying is not the biggest loss of life; disappearing while living is a very big loss of life, and I don't want to do that under any circumstances. So now I am a free bird, and I am living my own life, which I enjoy.

Yes, I dream very big. Even if I don't reach the moon, it's okay; we will reach the sky because now I know that weakness is our time, not the person. Today there is a lot of trouble, but tomorrow there will be success because our Bhagavad Gita says that when times are bad, and you endure that time, only that person who endures can become something in the future.

To understand where my fault lay, I kept wondering, but then I realised, "Kripa, you alone are enough." Yes, you've already been through so much in your life. Leaving a place where people don't value or respect you is the right thing to do. Strong women simply ignore and move forward with their lives. Peti told me to forget what happened, saying she had always suspected that Roy might do this someday. Peti and Tesi advised me well, and Stacey always gave me good advice. And yes, my mom supported me with the best advice, always there for me.

When I talked to my mom, she assured me that she didn't think Roy would break off the relationship with me in this way, especially given how well he used to talk to her. My whole family liked him. But what was meant to happen happened, and no one could stop it. I was shattered inside, though. It's easy to explain things to others, but only those who go through such experiences truly understand the depth of that pain. Peti kept me close, always taking me out because she knew how I would cope. But now, I had to get used to living without Roy. It's challenging to convince your heart to move on, especially when someone you've gotten used to talking to every morning and evening suddenly cuts off all communication. It's hard.

Tesi, Peti, and I understood each other well since we'd all been through similar times. Peti had always told me she didn't trust Roy, but I was in love and trusted him completely. This even led to some arguments between us, though I knew Peti wanted the best for me. She's a true, loyal friend. I started keeping myself busy with work, focusing on my responsibilities. We celebrated the nine days of Navratri, where I would fast.

In the evenings, Diya would take me along with her to dance and celebrate the cultural festivities. I would go, but my heart wasn't in it because my mind was still on Roy. Even though we'd recently broken up, Diya encouraged me to join the celebrations and dance. My mind would focus on it for a while, but soon enough, my thoughts would drift back to Roy.

Inside, I didn't feel happy about anything, but I had no choice but to carry on. I was determined not to let myself fall back into depression because I'd been there before, and I knew how difficult it was to come out of it. My mom, Peti, and Stacey were always there, supporting me with conversations and advice. Gradually, as I focused on work, my mind began to stabilise, although thoughts of Roy still lingered at times. My mom was not just my mother but also my friend and my idol. She is my god, especially after my divorce, as she's stood by me like a pillar, helping me in every possible way. Whenever I went to India, whether it was for shopping or tickets, she took care of everything. Without her, I don't know how I would have lived my life. And, of course, there's my daughter and my friends Peti, Yesh, and Diya, who have been here with me.

33). I had to come here because Roy was supposed to come to the USA. He needed to apply for a fiancée visa, and after I arrived here, about two weeks passed. I discussed everything with him, and he gave me all the important papers I needed for his application. Then, one day, I asked him a necessary question, and I don't know what happened, but he got angry with me. I asked him if he felt it wasn't working out between us, he should let me know. He said, "No, it's nothing like that. It's just that after my mom's death, my mind hasn't been in a good place, and you know that." And I knew that well because he was very close to his mother. But what happened had already happened and couldn't be changed. So, we just had to move forward.

Peti often told me that she knew his mother had passed, but that didn't mean he could take his anger out whenever he felt like it. I told her that he was just upset, and I knew he loved me deeply. I needed some important papers from him, which he was a bit late in providing. Before I knew it, a whole year had passed, and I hadn't even realised it. I was also very busy with work here. Tesi, Peti, and I worked together well, and Stacey was also very supportive. After returning from India, I asked if Peti was adjusting here, and she started to like it a bit more. Some time passed, and Peti's husband also came here from Arizona.

After coming back from India, I felt unsettled because of Roy, as he was there while I was here. We had only recently been together, so obviously, I didn't feel great. I also got busy with work, and then I asked Stacey how Peti was doing at work. Peti was, of course, very competent at her job. While I was in India, Stacey had taken very good care of Peti. She even took her to a restaurant to make her feel at home, and that night was also wonderful. Both Stacey and I are single moms; Stacey has a son named Corlo, who is a really nice boy. Stacey has also been through a tough time. Peti, Tesi, and I got along very well.

After about a week of my return from India, the three of us went out to an Indian restaurant because my friends knew I was a bit upset. Leaving Roy in India and coming back had made me feel down. My friends took me out to the restaurant, and we ate there, after which I got back to work. It was important to focus on work, and we had a lot of fun and laughs together at work.

Peti's life improved after moving to Texas. Her husband became much more loving, and both she and her husband got jobs at Home Depot. Meanwhile, we were working at the hotel and were happy with it. The three of us friends shared everything with each other—what was happening in our lives, good and bad, and even the smallest details. Our time together was enjoyable and much needed because everyone has their own stress in life. Sitting with that stress does nothing but make life miserable, so it's better to work, laugh, and have fun, in my opinion. Whether you do it happily or while crying, work has to be done regardless; you don't have a choice. In this world, no one is ready to help, so we have to stand up for ourselves.

Peti, Stacey, and I were a team, and I enjoyed teamwork. We understood each other well, and our team was strong. However, some of the housekeeping staff we worked with often had issues with Peti and me—likely because we were from different states. Stacey was local, but Peti and I seemed to be the targets. I never really understood why, as I was just doing my job and asking others to do theirs. Some people didn't appreciate that, wondering, "Who does she think she is, telling me what to do?" But we ignored it.

Peti and I would often go to Walmart for supplies, and one day, we went to Costco for hotel shopping. We borrowed Yesh's car, and after doing all the shopping, I was driving back. It was actually our first time at Costco, so I didn't set up the directions in the car's GPS. On our way back, I accidentally had a minor accident with an 18-wheeler truck. Fortunately, neither of us was hurt; we didn't even have a scratch, although the impact was a bit of a shock since it was such a large truck.

The main thing I worried about was Yesh's car. When I called Yesh to tell him about the accident, the first thing he asked was, "Are you and Peti okay? Did either of you get hurt?" He reassured me, saying not to worry about the car at all. I drove us back, and the car was quite damaged at the rear and side. Later, Yesh called again just to ask if Peti and I were alright. I've rarely met anyone like Yesh, who cared more about us than about his car. Most people here would worry more about their car than anyone else's well-being, but Yesh was a unique boss who genuinely cared about us.

When we returned to the hotel, I told Stacey about the accident, and her reaction was similar—she asked if we were okay, and then looked at the car. Later, Yesh simply got a new car, but I still felt a bit guilty since I was driving and it was his car. I even called Ganesh and told him what happened, and he said, "It's okay; a car can be replaced, but once a life is lost, it never comes back." And it's so true; in this world, we can replace anything, but life, once gone, can never return. Thankfully, neither of us was hurt—that was the important thing.

One day, Peti and I went shopping at Walmart, and as always, whenever we were together, we'd have so much fun. This time, we accidentally stood at the exit door, waiting for it to open. A young man passed us, went to the entrance, and it was then that we realised our mistake! People were laughing at us, and we couldn't help but laugh at ourselves too. Everywhere we went, Peti and I managed to create these silly moments that made us laugh. Work hours flew by, and I hardly noticed the time passing. Every day, I'd talk to Roy in the morning and evening, sometimes for hours. He'd gradually send me all the information I needed for his application, and before we knew it, a year had passed.

Then, in July, on the anniversary of Roy's mother's passing, something happened—I still don't know why, but he got angry with me. Out of nowhere, he told me he didn't want to continue our relationship. Thankfully, I hadn't yet started the U.S. application for him, or else I would have felt even worse. At first, I wondered if he'd only acted lovingly to come here, but then I dismissed that thought, as he wasn't that kind of person. To this day, I don't fully understand why he ended our relationship. Life has so many questions that remain unanswered. Yes, thoughts about why and how it happened cross my mind, but those questions never lead anywhere—they just remain incomplete.

Many times, I'd feel like calling him, to ask where I went wrong, but then I'd remind myself that *I am enough on my own*. If someone doesn't value or respect you, leaving is the right choice. A strong woman simply ignores and moves forward in her life.

www.ingramcontent.com/pod-product-compliance
Lightning Source LLC
Chambersburg PA
CBHW071437300726
48976CB00004B/1357